THE HORROR OF
DUNWICK FARM

Also by Dan Smith:

The Invasion of Crooked Oak

The Beast of Harwood Forest

THE HORROR OF
DUNWICK FARM

DAN SMITH

Illustrated by
Chris King

Barrington Stoke

For Lennox and Theo

First published in 2022 in Great Britain by
Barrington Stoke Ltd
18 Walker Street, Edinburgh, EH3 7LP

www.barringtonstoke.co.uk

Text © 2022 Dan Smith
Illustrations © 2022 Chris King

A CIP catalogue record for this book is available
from the British Library upon request

ISBN: 978-1-80090-083-7

Printed by Hussar Books, Poland

CONTENTS

CHAPTER 1

Crash

"Rats!" said Mrs Hudson, the Biology teacher.

A picture of a black rat appeared on the whiteboard. The rat was sitting on a sewage pipe, rubbing its front paws together. It had yellow front teeth and a long tail that curved behind it like a fat worm.

"Ugh," Krish said with a shiver. "Gross."

The sleepy kids in the Year Eight Biology class laughed.

"What's wrong?" said Pete, who was sitting beside Krish, his best friend. "It's just a big mouse. It's cute."

"Cute?" Krish adjusted his glasses. He looked at Pete as if he'd just said he liked to eat slugs.

"Rats are an example of an 'invasive species'," said Mrs Hudson. "Who remembers what that means?" She glared at Pete. "How about you, Pete Brundle?"

"Umm," Pete started. "It's …" He brushed his mop of blond hair away from his forehead and smiled. "It's the last lesson of the day, Miss, and my brain isn't working properly. I've forgotten."

Mrs Hudson sighed and shook her head at Pete.

Nancy Finney raised her hand. Nancy was short and skinny, with hair the colour of autumn leaves. She was the smartest person in Year Eight.

"An 'invasive species'," Nancy said, "is an animal that's brought to a place by humans and ends up causing harm."

"Exactly," said Mrs Hudson. "Rats were originally only found in Asia, but they boarded ships in the past and spread. Now we find them all over the world, carrying diseases and causing harm to other animals." She paused. "I wonder if anyone can think of another example of an 'invasive species'?"

"Rabbits?" Nancy suggested. "Someone took rabbits from England to Australia and they ended up—"

Nancy was interrupted by the spluttering of a loud engine.

Everyone looked towards the open window. There was nothing to see except the school hall opposite. But the coughing, stuttering sound grew louder and louder, as if something were going to smash right into the classroom.

"We're going to die!" one of the boys screamed. Kids started to panic, pushing their chairs away from their desks.

"Stay calm!" Mrs Hudson shouted. "Stay calm!"

Pete, Nancy and Krish hurried to the window, searching for the cause of the terrible noise, but saw nothing.

"Sounds like it's going that way," Nancy said, and pointed towards the centre of the village.

Whatever it was, it passed overhead with a deafening rumble that rattled the glass of the windows. Then the sound faded, chugging away into the distance.

A few moments later, there was a tremendous crash.

Krish was sure he felt the ground shake.

CHAPTER 2

Roadblock

The bell rang for the end of the lesson and everyone raced into the corridor to talk about what had happened.

"It was a plane crash!" said Stephen Blatty from Year Nine. He was fighting his way past the sweaty crowd, trying to make it to the stairs.

"How do you know?" Nancy shouted over the excited chatter that rolled along the corridor like a tidal wave.

"I saw it," Stephen boasted. "We were doing games on the field when it went over. Looks like it crashed on the other side of the village."

Pete, Nancy and Krish stuck together as they made their way past the crowd and down the stairs to the main hallway. An army of teachers was trying to keep everyone calm.

"Come on!" Pete said to Nancy and Krish, urging them to keep up as he fought his way out into the warm, bright afternoon. They hurried past the bus waiting to take kids home to remote villages and went straight to the bike racks.

"We have to go and check it out," Pete said. "A plane crash! How awesome is that?"

"Awesome?" Krish wondered out loud as he unlocked his bike. "Only if no one got hurt."

"Yeah," Pete agreed. "Of course."

The three of them jumped on their bikes and headed out of the gates, along with every other kid who cycled to school. There was a whole crowd of them riding through the village of Crooked Oak, all headed in the direction Stephen Blatty said the plane had come down.

It wasn't long before they were out of the village and speeding along Harper Road, a narrow country lane with wide fields on each side. The smell of manure wafted on the breeze.

"Do you think the plane blew up?" Pete said, unable to hide his excitement. "I can't see any smoke."

"Not everything blows up when it crashes," Krish said. He was panting as he tried to keep up with Pete and Nancy.

On the bend further up the road, kids on bikes were slowing down and bunching together. There were cars there, parked on the grass verge next to the drystone wall.

Krish came closer and spotted an orange barrier. Parked behind it was a black van with tinted windows, blocking the road. There was a black Range Rover too, with a man and a woman standing beside it wearing dark suits and staring at the crowd.

"Typical," Pete said as they reached the crowd. "The most exciting thing to happen in Crooked Oak for ages and we can't even get a good look."

Pete pushed past the other kids to get close to the barrier, but the woman stepped forward. Without a word, she held up a hand and scowled at Pete.

"That's weird," Pete said, moving back.

"That's not the only thing," Nancy replied. "Look over there."

Over the top of the drystone wall, they could just see the far end of the field in the distance. They had been expecting to see a crashed plane, but instead there was a large white tent. Beside it were more black vehicles like the ones blocking the road.

"That's the kind of tent you see on the news," Krish said. "When the police are hiding a murder scene."

"Except there *aren't* any police," Nancy said. "Or ambulances."

Krish scanned the field. "You're right. None at all."

"But something must have crashed," Pete said. "Look at the trees."

Right behind the tent, the field backed onto a wood. The tops of some of the trees were damaged as if something had smashed into them.

"Why are they hiding it?" Nancy asked. "Why cover it with a big tent?"

"Maybe there's something on the news," Krish said, and pulled out his phone. He turned it on and frowned. "No signal." He held his phone up to find a signal and noticed other people doing the same thing.

"The signal normally works here," Nancy said.

"Well, it doesn't now," Krish replied.

"It's a UFO," Pete said with certainty. "A UFO has crashed and they're trying to keep it secret. Think about it. They've covered it with a tent, they've blocked the phone signal and there are black cars everywhere. It's a classic UFO cover-up."

Nancy and Krish glanced at each other. They rolled their eyes and burst out laughing.

"What?" Pete asked.

"UFOs?" Krish said. "Seriously?"

"*Something's* going on," Pete insisted. "Hey, this could be a story for the Mystery Shed."

The Mystery Shed was their favourite website. It was full of stories about strange and unexplained events – from monsters and mind-controlling fungi, to disappearing ships and strange lights in the sky.

"If only we could get a better look at it," Pete said as he squinted across the field.

"Maybe we can," Krish said. "My house is on the other side of those woods. I've got an idea."

CHAPTER 3

Dunwick Farm

Pete, Nancy and Krish jumped on their bikes and left the crowd behind. Twenty minutes later they arrived at Dunwick Farm, where Krish lived.

Dunwick Farm was a large house with a cobbled yard in front of it. At one side of the yard stood a run-down barn that was out of bounds because it was dangerous. Krish didn't like going near it anyway because it was creepy and probably full of rats. On the other side of the yard was a row of old brick outhouses. The whole farm was in a terrible condition, but

Krish's dad was a builder and he'd bought it to do it up.

At the moment, the only animals on the farm were five chickens, four goats and the family dog – an Australian Kelpie called Gizmo. Gizmo spotted Krish and his friends arriving and raced across the yard in a blur of brown fur. He ran around Krish's bike, trying to bite the front tyre.

Krish's mum was still at work, but in the yard was his younger sister, Rashmi, helping their dad unload chicken feed from the back of their pick-up truck. She ran over as Krish and his friends climbed off their bikes and leaned them against the house.

"Hey, Nancy," Rashmi said, adjusting her messy ponytail.

Nancy smiled. "Hey."

"Did you hear about the plane?" Rashmi asked. "It crashed in the field on the other side of the wood. I—"

"We heard about it," Krish interrupted his sister. "You can leave us alone now."

"Don't be mean," Nancy told him.

"I'm not being mean,'" Krish said. "I just don't want her hanging around. Come on, this way."

Krish led Pete and Nancy around the back of the house, past the goat pen and into an overgrown field of long grass bordered by a rickety fence. At the far end was a thick wood.

"Hey!" Rashmi said, following them. "Are you going into the woods to see the crash? Can I come? Dad wouldn't let—"

"No." Krish cut his sister off and glared at her.

"Please?" Rashmi asked. "I promise not to tell them how much gel you use to make the front of your hair stick up."

"I don't mind if she comes," Nancy said with a shrug.

"Yeah, what harm can it do?" Pete agreed. "Gel head."

Krish sighed and said to Rashmi, "Fine. But don't get in the way."

They hurried across the field while Gizmo ran circles around them, getting under their feet. Krish kept telling him to "stay", but Gizmo was too excited for that.

It was easy to climb the fence at the far end of the field. In moments, they were in the woods surrounded by the sweet scent of spring flowers.

"This way," Krish said, leading his friends through the ancient trees. They reached a beck of clear, cold water and picked their way across the stepping stones. Gizmo jumped in, splashing and biting the bubbles. After that, it was a short hike to the far end of the woods, where some of the trees were damaged from the crash. From there they could see something white beyond the leaves.

Krish squatted down and put an arm around Gizmo to keep him still. The fur on Gizmo's neck was soft and warm and smelled like outdoors. The light brown stripe on Gizmo's head wrinkled as he looked up at Krish.

"There it is," Krish said. "That's the tent."

CHAPTER 4

A Kind of Madness

The huge white tent stood in the field like an alien monument surrounded by black vans and Range Rovers. Three people waited by the vehicles, dressed in smart dark suits.

Watching from the trees, Krish checked his phone while trying to hold Gizmo still. "No signal," he whispered.

"I bet they're blocking it," Pete told him. "There's something weird going on."

Nancy nudged Pete and pointed. "Someone's coming out," she said.

The front of the tent lifted up and two people emerged, dressed from head to foot in black protective outfits. Helmets, boots, gloves and bodysuits. Between them they carried a large zip-up bag.

"That's ..." Krish said, hesitating "... a body-bag."

"Someone must have been hurt," Nancy said. She opened the video app on her phone and started recording.

"But why are they wearing those outfits?" Pete wondered. "Maybe it's some kind of virus?"

"Those aren't hazmat suits," Krish said. "It looks more like armour."

In the field, the two people in protective outfits lifted the body-bag into the back of one of the vans and slammed the doors shut. They returned to the tent, lifted the entrance flap

and ducked back inside, giving a brief glimpse of what was hidden underneath.

"Did you see that?" Krish said.

"A small plane," Nancy said, quickly zooming in with her phone. "There's some kind of marking on it. A number, I think."

A few moments later, the people in protective gear came out again. They were each carrying a glass tank about the size of a shoebox, which they placed in the back of a Range Rover.

"Is there something moving in those tanks?" Rashmi asked, squinting to see better.

"Like aliens, you mean?" Pete suggested.

"Not everything is aliens or vampires," Nancy said.

"Yeah, but maybe this time it is," Pete replied. "Maybe—"

Without warning, Gizmo let out a long, low growl. Everyone looked down at him as he tensed in Krish's grip and the dark brown hairs on the back of his neck stood up. Gizmo bared his teeth and growled again.

"What's the matter, Giz?" Rashmi said. She put a hand on him, but Gizmo snapped his teeth around the hem of Krish's coat and pulled so hard that Krish almost fell over.

"Gizmo!" Krish tried to calm him down. "What are you doing?"

Gizmo let go of Krish's coat and stood with his ears pricked up, barking loudly as if there were something right in front of him. Something that scared him.

"Stop!" Krish told him. "They'll hear!"

"Too late," Pete said. "They already have."

Close by in the field, the men and women in dark suits turned to look at the woods. Vehicle doors opened and people climbed out to scan the area. One of them pointed towards the trees where Krish and the others were hiding.

"Let's get out of here," Nancy said.

Gizmo was the first to run, scampering away into the undergrowth. Krish and the others followed. They raced past the trees, leapt across the beck and climbed the fence back into the field at Dunwick Farm. They only slowed down when they were halfway across the field, glancing back and panting hard from the effort of running.

"They didn't see us," Pete said. "We're too good for them."

But their relief was short-lived. They trudged past the goat pen at the top of the field and the goats began to scream. It was the most awful sound. Like a thousand tortured souls all calling out at the same time.

"Blimey!" Nancy said, shocked. "What's wrong with them?"

"I don't know," Krish told her. "That's what they do when they're scared."

"Well, they're scaring me," Nancy replied, picking up her pace. She was eager to escape the awful noise, but as they came near the chicken run by the barn, the hens began squawking. On the barn roof, a pair of magpies hopped about, chattering angrily.

Krish and his friends stopped in the yard and looked at one another. All around them, the air was filled with the sound of scared animals.

It was as if a kind of madness had fallen over Dunwick Farm.

CHAPTER 5

AREA 51

That evening, Krish was alone inside one of the old brick outhouses at Dunwick Farm. It smelled damp in there, but his dad had fitted a grey carpet and painted the stone walls white so Krish and his friends could use it. He had even bought them some brightly coloured beanbags and given them a kettle. There was a desk with an old PC and a printer, and Krish had decorated the walls with posters. Pete had made a sign for the front door that said "AREA 51".

Gizmo was asleep in his basket in the corner. Krish's phone buzzed just as he was putting up a poster of a flying saucer hovering over some trees. He grabbed the phone and flopped into a red beanbag to read the message on the AREA 51 group chat.

NANCY: I got a screenshot from my video.

A blurry photo of the white tent appeared. Krish could see the tail end of a small plane hidden beneath it. The tail was light blue, with a white stripe and a series of numbers in black.

NANCY: I researched it and you'll never guess what?

PETE: It's a UFO?

NANCY: No, you doofus, it's a plane. Those numbers are its registration. And there's a story about it on the Mystery Shed.

PETE: What? Already?

NANCY: It's a story from a few years ago. Check this out.

A link popped up and Krish tapped on it to see a Mystery Shed article titled "What's Going On?" It was about a company called BGen that was doing medical research in a lab in a remote part of Northumberland, using illegal exotic animals. The article had a photo of a small airfield in front of a large grey concrete building without any windows. A small plane stood on the airfield. The numbers on its tail were the same as the numbers on the crashed plane.

KRISH: Maybe the plane was going to that building when it crashed.

NANCY: But what was it taking there?

PETE: A virus, maybe? Remember what they were wearing?

KRISH: Those suits looked more like armour. And what were those glass tanks they were carrying?

More importantly, Krish thought, *why were the animals on the farm so scared? And—*

BANG! The door to AREA 51 flew open with a crash.

CHAPTER 6

Something in the Dark

Krish dropped his phone and Gizmo leapt to his feet as Rashmi barged into AREA 51.

"Mum says you have to come in now," said Rashmi.

"Oh my god!" Krish shouted. "You nearly gave me a heart attack! You're supposed to knock."

"Whatever." Rashmi pulled a face. "Mum says dinner's ready, so if you're not quick, I'm having your paratha. And don't forget to put the bin out. It's the blue bin tomorrow."

"It's *your* turn," Krish said.

"No it's not." Rashmi ran back to the house, leaving Krish standing in the open doorway, staring out into the night.

It had been a sunny spring day, but now it was cold and dark, and Krish could see his own breath. On the other side of the yard, the wheelie bins stood like demons in the damp shadows between the barn and the log pile, close to the chicken run. Krish shuddered at the thought of having to go over there. The log pile was always full of bugs and spiders, and he was sure he'd seen a rat there a few weeks ago.

He took a deep breath and said, "Come on, Gizmo." Then he left AREA 51 and crossed the yard towards the bins.

As he came closer, the security light clicked on above the barn door. A bright glow flooded across the log pile, lighting up the bins.

"At least that still works," Krish muttered.

But as he said it, there was a bright spark, a loud pop, and the light went out.

Krish stopped dead, waiting for his eyes to adjust to the dark. And in that moment, he saw something move in the shadows of the log pile.

Gizmo started to growl.

The hens let out a series of short, sharp clucks.

Krish stayed where he was, his heart beating faster. Gizmo edged away from the log pile, teeth bared. The hair on the back of his neck was bristling.

"What is it, Giz?" Krish whispered. "You see a rat?"

A sudden movement made Krish look back to the log pile. There was a rustling in the overgrown weeds beside it, then the hens began to squawk and flap about in their run.

Gizmo whined. He nudged Krish, barked once, then scampered back to the house and disappeared in the front door, which Rashmi had left open. Krish wished he could do the same but told himself to be brave. It was just a rat. Pete wouldn't be scared of a rat. Nor would Nancy.

Krish forced himself to stride forward and grab the handle of the blue wheelie bin. Without looking back, he quickly dragged the bin up to the front gate, then turned and ran straight for the house. The hens were still complaining, but Krish didn't care. As soon as he was inside the house, he slammed the door behind him and breathed a sigh of relief.

*

In bed that night, Krish dreamed of faceless people in protective suits. He also dreamed of large white tents and giant rats. And in the darkest hours, the sound of machinery drifted over the woods towards Dunwick Farm.

CHAPTER 7

Exoskeleton

At school the next day, everyone was talking about the crash. But the weird thing was, the kids who came in by bus said the road was open again. The white tent was gone and the field was clear – as if nothing had happened.

"That must be what I heard last night," Krish told Nancy and Pete during form time. "They were clearing everything away."

"Who was?" Pete asked.

"BGen," Nancy suggested. "At least ... that's who I think the plane belongs to. And I looked them up last night after seeing that article on

the Mystery Shed. BGen is part of BioMesa –
the fracking company."

Krish pushed up his glasses.

"Here we go," Pete said. "Krish is in serious
mode."

"BioMesa does lots of things, not just
fracking," Krish said, ignoring Pete. "Oil, gas,
medical research. I looked them up too, but no
one knows exactly what they're doing in that
building here in Northumberland that Nancy
found out about. That's probably where the
plane was going."

"Is it far away?" Pete asked.

"Close to Harwood Forest," Krish said. "Too
far for us to go on our bikes, if that's what
you're thinking."

"Shame," Pete said. "There's definitely
something strange going on. A story for the

Mystery Shed. And the phone signal is being weird. Everyone's complaining about it. It hardly works."

"Yep," Nancy said. "Like you said, it's almost as if someone is blocking it."

*

Krish arrived home from school that afternoon to find his dad working in the yard, wearing blue overalls that bulged around his belly.

"Where's Gizmo?" Krish asked as he climbed off his bike and leaned it against the wall.

His dad looked around and shrugged. "Inside. I think something spooked him."

"Like what?" Krish wondered.

"Could be anything with that daft dog. Here, put those on." Krish's dad pointed to some overalls and an orange hard hat lying in his wheelbarrow.

Krish groaned. "Seriously? I've got homework to—"

"The fresh air will do you good," his dad said with a smile that made his moustache wriggle. "Give your brain a rest for half an hour. You can do your homework afterwards." He put the hard hat on Krish's head and knocked on it with his fist.

"What about Rashmi?" Krish asked. "Doesn't she have to help?"

"Already on it!" Rashmi said, appearing from around the back of the house carrying a bucket of chicken feed. "What's wrong? Worried the hard hat will spoil your hair?"

Krish sighed and pulled the overalls on top of his school uniform.

"This'll cheer you up," his dad said, handing Krish the weed-burner.

The weed-burner was a narrow metal pipe with a wide perforated barrel at one end and a handle at the other. A gas canister was clipped just below the handle. Basically, it was a mini flame-thrower.

"Want me to remind you how it works?" his dad asked.

"I think I've got it," Krish said. He pointed the end at the ground and turned the valve to switch on the gas. He thumbed the striker switch and a soft yellow flame ignited at the wide end.

"Be safe," his dad said.

"Of course." Krish pressed the trigger and the soft yellow flame turned into a fierce blue cone of fire. He couldn't help grinning. Pete would *love* this.

Krish was busy scorching the weeds around the barn when he heard magpies cackling a warning. He stopped to watch them hopping about on the battered roof. Whatever had upset them was unsettling the hens too. They weren't feasting on the grain Rashmi had put out, but had retreated to the hen house, where they were making soft growling noises.

Krish scanned the yard and was about to go back to burning the weeds when something caught his eye.

A dead spider hung from a rusty nail in the barn wall, twisting gently in the breeze. It was almost colourless, with its legs curled inwards and a body at least as big as the size of Krish's thumb.

"Hey, Dad!" Krish called. "Come and look at this!"

A moment later, his dad and Rashmi came to see what Krish was shouting about.

"It's massive." Krish pointed at the spider with the end of the weed burner.

Rashmi leaned closer for a good look. "Are you scared of spiders?" she teased. "You're scared of everything. It's not even alive. I bet *Pete* wouldn't be scared of a dead spider."

"I'm not scared," Krish said. "I just ... don't like spiders."

"That's what people always say when they're scared of spiders," Rashmi said. *"I just don't like spiders,"* she added, imitating her brother's voice.

"Shut up!" Krish shoved his sister. "It's a *big* spider."

"House spiders *can* be big," his dad said. "And you know that's not a *dead* spider, don't

you? It's just a husk. An exoskeleton. Spiders shed their skins when they grow."

Krish shuddered. "So the spider that shed this skin is even bigger now?" he asked.

"Massive," Rashmi said, standing on her tiptoes to whisper in Krish's ear. "And it knows where you live!"

When his dad and Rashmi went back to work, Krish pointed the weed-burner at the spider husk and pressed the trigger. He watched the husk singe around the edges, then catch fire and burn away to nothing.

He hoped he would never meet the spider that had left it behind.

CHAPTER 8

A Strange Silence

Of all the seasons, Krish liked spring best of all. It was especially lovely on the farm, because he woke every morning to the dawn chorus of blackbirds, robins and wrens.

But when Krish woke on Thursday morning, he was greeted by the sound of his dad's pick-up truck grumbling as he left for work, followed by an eerie stillness. Later, Krish took his bike from the shelter at the back of the house and the farm was deadly silent. His mum and Rashmi had already left, the hens and goats weren't making a sound, and there wasn't

the slightest hint of birdsong. Even the noisy
magpies were nowhere to be seen.

It was as if Dunwick Farm was holding its
breath.

*

Krish waited for Pete and Nancy outside
King's Corner Shop in Crooked Oak. Kids were
everywhere, bustling in and out of the shop,
buying sweets and cans of drink before school.
They ran about and joked and showed each
other memes on their phones. The air smelled
like bubblegum. Every so often, an adult would
walk past and tut loudly.

Krish pulled his bike onto the pavement and
scanned the notices in the shop window.

"Anything interesting?" A voice spoke in
his ear and Krish turned to see Pete standing
behind him.

"Yes," said Nancy, appearing from the crowd of kids. "Look." She pointed to a poster in the shop window that showed a black-and-white picture of a missing cat. The name "Mr Jingles" was written underneath, along with a description and an address and telephone number.

"So?" Pete said, shrugging.

"You need to be more observant," Nancy said, using her phone to take a photo of the missing-cat poster. "Come and have a look at this."

Nancy led Krish and Pete along the pavement, weaving their bikes among the other kids until they reached Hooper's Village Shop.

"See?" Nancy said, stopping in front of the shop window. "Another missing-cat poster. But for a different cat."

Krish adjusted his glasses and leaned closer. Nancy was right. This one was for a cat called Henry.

"And there's another one," Nancy said, pointing to a poster on the lamp post behind them.

"Cats are going missing?" Pete wondered.

"They're not the only things disappearing," Krish said. "I mean, where did all the birds go? The farm was silent this morning – it was like nothing dared make a sound."

"There are birds on my street," Pete told him. "They woke me up."

"Same on Elm Street," Nancy agreed.

"There's something else," Krish said. "Gizmo is being weird. He won't leave the house unless he *has* to. It's like he's scared of something."

Pete frowned. "It's something to do with that plane, isn't it? Aliens maybe? Or vampires?"

Krish sighed and shook his head. "You always say that. It's *never* vampires."

"Come on, we'll be late for school," Nancy said.

But Krish couldn't focus at school that day. He couldn't stop thinking about the birds.

*

That night, Krish woke to noise and confusion.

He sat up with a start, blood pounding in his ears as he looked around blindly in the darkness. From outside, he heard a loud and terrifying screaming. Downstairs, Gizmo was barking in response. Upstairs, there was movement in the house, a deep voice speaking, then light glowed under Krish's door.

Krish went to the door. He opened it just enough to peer out and see his dad on the landing, pulling on his scruffy Chewbacca dressing gown.

"Dad?" Krish whispered.

"It's the goats," his dad said sleepily. "I'd better go and check."

The thought of going outside filled Krish with dread, but he had to be brave. It was what Pete would do.

"I'll come," Krish said, grabbing his dressing gown.

His mum and Rashmi followed them downstairs, turning on all the lights. They waited in the kitchen with Gizmo while Krish and his dad grabbed their wellies from the mat by the back door.

Krish's dad turned his boots upside down and gave them a shake before putting them on. When Krish did the same, he jumped back in alarm as something large fell out of his boot. It hit the floor with a solid "plop" and rushed away under the cooker.

"Oh my god!" Krish said, his heart beating even faster than before. "What was that? Was that a spider? It was huge!"

Gizmo whined and ran out of the room.

"Forget it," his dad said. "We need to go."

They switched on their torches and headed out into the cold night, but Krish glanced back at the cooker. He had the most horrible feeling that something was sitting in the darkness beneath it, watching him.

CHAPTER 9

Fear in the Night

The awful screaming echoed around the farm as Krish and his dad waded through the long grass towards the goat pen.

The grass inside the pen was cropped short, eaten by the goats. In the flickering torchlight, Krish saw two goats running in circles, while a third reared up on its back legs, stamping its front hooves on the ground. The fourth goat lay on its side, shuddering.

"What's the matter?" Krish's dad spoke to them with a soothing voice. "What's all the fuss?"

Krish stepped closer and suddenly saw strange trails appearing in the long grass around the pen.

It was as if something small and close to the ground was running away from him and his dad. Then he caught a glimpse of long, spindly legs flickering in the light.

"There's something in the grass," Krish whispered as he swept the beam of his torch around him. "What *was* that?"

"Rats," his dad said. "They must've been bothering the goats."

But Krish didn't think they had looked like rats.

His dad went right up to the pen and spoke to the goats. Eventually they calmed down and he was able to go into the pen and check on the goat lying on its side.

Krish's dad knelt beside it for a while, then looked back at Krish.

"I think it's dead," he said.

CHAPTER 10

Coma

They waited ages for the vet to come. When she finally arrived, she told them the goat wasn't dead but in some sort of coma, as if it had fallen into a deep sleep. She couldn't tell them any more than that, so she took the goat away to keep an eye on it.

Krish hardly slept after that, so he was exhausted the next morning when he headed out for school. He cycled along the narrow country road in a daze – until he was shocked by the wailing of sirens. A moment later an ambulance came around the corner and raced towards him, lights flashing.

Krish pulled his bike over onto the grass verge and watched the ambulance pass him. It turned down the drive to Rose Cottage, where Mrs Hudson their Biology teacher lived. The ambulance screeched to a halt, then the paramedics jumped out and rushed inside Rose Cottage.

Feeling wide awake now, Krish waited a few minutes to see what was happening, but everything was quiet. He waited a while longer, then checked the time and realised he was going to be late for school.

He was disappointed that he couldn't find out any more but pushed down on the bike pedals and cycled away.

*

At break-time, Pete, Nancy and Krish were sitting at the edge of the playing field behind the main school building.

"Mrs Hudson's in hospital," Nancy said. "In a coma. I heard some of the Year Nines talking about it in the corridor earlier."

"A coma?" Krish asked, pushing his glasses up his nose. "That's what the vet said about our goat."

"That's weird, right?" Pete said. He plucked a blade of grass and put it in his mouth, then lay back and stared at the clear sky. "Birds not singing. Goats and Biology teachers in comas. Cats going missing. The phone signal not working properly. There's a Mystery Shed story screaming at us."

"But what is it?" Nancy asked. "What's going on in Crooked Oak?"

*

For the second time that week, Krish couldn't focus on lessons. He was too tired and had too many things on his mind. After school, he headed home with so many thoughts spinning around his head that he almost didn't spot the black Range Rover parked on the drive at Rose Cottage. He caught a glimpse of it through gaps in the fence lining Mrs Hudson's drive, but it took a moment to realise what it was. Only then did he press hard on his brakes and his bike screeched to a halt.

The road was quiet. The fields on each side were empty of the usual birdlife.

Krish waited, watching the Range Rover on the other side of Mrs Hudson's fence. It was the same kind of vehicle as the ones he had seen at the crash site. After a moment, Krish looked both ways along the road, then wheeled his bike onto the grass verge and took out his phone to message Pete and Nancy.

No signal again.

Frustrated, Krish grunted and put away his phone. He adjusted his glasses, imagining that Pete would say he should go and have a look – that he should find out what was going on. Nancy would probably agree with him.

But what if he got caught?

You're scared of everything! Rashmi's words came back to haunt him.

"Pete wouldn't be scared," Krish muttered to himself.

But Pete was *always* the bravest.

Krish squeezed his eyes shut and made a decision. He couldn't believe he was going to do this on his own.

CHAPTER 11

Monstrosity

Krish hid his bike and crept along the drive to Rose Cottage. There was no sign of movement from the Range Rover, but he heard voices drifting from the back garden. Krish took a deep breath to calm his nerves, then sneaked along the path at the side of the cottage. He reached the end of the path and spotted two people standing on the back lawn. He ducked behind a large shrub to watch them.

The man and woman were dressed from head to toe in the same protective outfits Krish had seen people wearing at the crash site. Suits, masks and gloves. Between them on the grass was a duffel bag from which the woman lifted a glass tank about the size of a shoebox. They nodded to each other, then went to the large shed at the bottom of the garden. The man eased open the door and began to remove everything from the shed as if he was searching for something. He worked slowly and carefully, without saying a word to the woman, who waited with the glass tank in her arms.

Before long, the lawn was cluttered with a lawnmower, spades, a gardening fork and—

"OH GOD!" the man shouted from inside the shed.

The shock made Krish want to turn and run, but he forced himself to stay and watch as the man slowly backed out of the shed.

The man nodded to the woman holding the tank, then she took a deep breath and headed inside. She rummaged about inside the shed and came out a few minutes later. Then the man and woman ripped off their masks and stood catching their breath.

"Is this it?" the man said as the woman held up the glass tank. "Please let this be Subject Zero."

The woman studied it closely. She was blocking Krish's view of the tank, so it was impossible for him to see what was inside.

"I'm afraid not," the woman said. "This is its offspring."

"They hatched already?" The man sounded worried. "My god, they'll be spreading out. How many do you think there are?"

"Hundreds," said the woman. "Maybe thousands. And they grow fast. But they're still young – they won't be too venomous ... yet. Our only chance is to find Subject Zero."

"How the hell are we going to do that?" the man replied.

"Keep watching the hospitals," the woman said. "Check the local vets." She peered into the glass tank. "There's so much we don't know about it. Beautiful, isn't it?"

"Beautiful?" the man said. "It's a *monstrosity*. And its mother is on the loose."

The woman shook her head. "She'll be hiding somewhere dark and sheltered. We'll find her." As she said it, the woman turned around and Krish caught a glimpse of what was in the glass tank.

It was a spider.

CHAPTER 12

Arachnophobia

As soon as Krish was home, he connected to Wi-Fi and texted Pete and Nancy to come and meet him in AREA 51. They cycled into Dunwick Farm later that evening. Rashmi was in the yard practising on her skateboard and Gizmo was lying by the house.

Rashmi popped the skateboard into the air and caught it with one hand, then ran over. Gizmo barked once in greeting but stayed where he was.

"Hey, Nancy!" Rashmi called.

"You're getting good at that," Nancy said as she and Pete climbed off their bikes.

Rashmi smiled and looked embarrassed. Before she could say anything, the door to AREA 51 creaked open and Krish looked out, scowling at her.

"Stop annoying Nancy," he said. "It's bad enough I have to look after you while Mum and Dad are out."

"You don't have to 'look after' me," Rashmi said.

"Whatever." Krish glared at her, then looked at Pete and Nancy. "Come in – there's something I need to tell you."

"We can play cricket if you like?" Rashmi called as Nancy and Pete headed into AREA 51. "I'll get my bat and—"

"No," Krish growled at her.

"You don't have to be so mean to your sister," Nancy said when Krish closed the door to AREA 51.

"She's a pain," Krish told Nancy. "Anyway, forget about her." Krish recounted what he had seen at Rose Cottage, telling Nancy and Pete everything about the man and the woman. And the spider.

As soon as he was finished, Nancy pulled out her phone and started tapping on the screen.

"A *spider?*" Pete cringed. "Are you sure that's what you saw?"

"I'm positive," Krish said. "But it looked weird. I mean ... it was big and it was a funny colour. Pale. Like grey, maybe, or almost see-through.

"Ugh." Pete shuddered.

"Wait," Nancy said, glancing up from her phone. "You're scared of spiders? The great Pete Brundle has arachnophobia?"

"Arachno-what?" Pete asked.

"Arachnophobia," Nancy said. "The fear of spiders. It's very common."

"I'm not scared of spiders," Pete protested. "I just don't like them."

"Sure," Nancy said sarcastically, and went back to looking at her phone.

"Those people at Rose Cottage looked scared," Krish said quietly. "They kept talking about 'Subject Zero' and about something 'hatching' and 'spreading out'."

"Oh my god," Pete mumbled. He got up from his beanbag and looked around, checking the corners of AREA 51. When he was close to the door, Rashmi barged in and Pete almost jumped out of his skin.

"You're supposed to knock!" Krish snapped at Rashmi.

"I heard noises," Rashmi said, ignoring Krish. "In the barn. We should go and look – it might be one of the missing cats."

"It's just rats," Krish told her. "And stay away from there – it's dangerous."

Rashmi frowned and said, "Well, can—"

"We're busy," Krish interrupted her. "Can't you just leave us alone for five minutes?"

Rashmi stared at him, then turned and stormed out. A moment later, they heard the sound of skateboard wheels in the yard outside.

"Ugh," Krish moaned. "She's so annoying."

"I've found something," Nancy said, looking up at him. "I think it's your spider."

CHAPTER 13

The Glass Spider

"I googled 'BGen' and 'spiders'," Nancy explained. "I found this article about caves in Brazil. Apparently, a deep cave system was uncovered when illegal gold miners cut down part of the rainforest. The cave had been isolated from the outside world for ... blimey ... five billion years!"

Krish whistled between his teeth. "That's a long time," he said.

"The environment in the cave is toxic," Nancy went on, quickly reading the article on her phone. "But they found insects and a larger predator – a spider. They nicknamed it the

'Glass Spider' because it's almost translucent. It doesn't have eyes but *does* have 'highly adapted sensory organs', which means it can hunt in total darkness."

"So the illegal miners went looking for gold and found a spider," Krish said.

"And not just any old spider," Nancy said. "This one is highly venomous. Some of the miners were killed by it!" Nancy looked up. "Serves them right. They shouldn't have been cutting down the rainforest."

"That's harsh," Pete said. He flopped into a yellow beanbag and tucked up his legs, glancing around the room nervously. Krish watched him, wondering if Pete really was scared of spiders. How did Krish not already know that?

"The Glass Spider is a social spider," Nancy continued. "They live in colonies of thousands—"

"Thousands?" Pete wrapped his arms around his knees.

"With a 'queen' at the centre of it all," Nancy finished. "They're aggressive and territorial, especially if the queen is threatened. They grow fast and have a short lifespan. Sometimes 'soldier' spiders fan out of the caves to hunt. They bite their prey to stun it, then take it back to the colony to be shared."

"Gross," Pete said. "Is that what you saw at Rose Cottage? Is that what was in Mrs Hudson's shed? A Glass Spider?'

"Maybe it escaped from the plane crash," Krish said.

"But why would they have spiders on that plane?" Pete wondered.

"Scientists from BGen think they can use the spider venom to make a medicine," Nancy said, still reading the article. "Something to

71

cure long-term pain. But environmentalists have blocked the caves to stop BGen from taking specimens."

"But they did, didn't they?" Krish stood up, excited. "They *did* take a specimen. They stole a spider and it was on that plane. They were taking it to that building here in Northumberland."

"But they caught it," Pete said. "You saw them catch it."

"I saw them catch *a* spider," Krish reminded him. "Not *the* spider. Not 'Subject Zero'. The woman at Rose Cottage said something about its 'offspring', so what if Subject Zero is a queen, like Nancy said? What if it got away when the plane crashed and now it's out there somewhere hatching 'soldiers'?" Krish pointed in the direction of the woods behind Dunwick Farm. "People should stop messing about with nature."

"But they took it for research," Pete said. "That makes it all right, doesn't it?"

"No way!" Nancy said.

"For relief from long-term pain, though," Pete went on, looking hurt.

"Oh," Krish said. He took off his glasses and rubbed his eyes. "Sorry. I didn't think." Pete's mum was desperate for a cure for her terrible back pain. On bad days she couldn't even walk, and Pete had to look after her a lot of the time.

"Yeah, I'm sorry too," Nancy said. "But now these dangerous spiders are out there doing goodness knows what. Think about it. Maybe Mrs Hudson got bitten. And what about those missing cats?"

"And the birds," Krish said. "I haven't seen or heard any birds around here for days."

"It could be an invasive species," Nancy said. "Like we learned about in Biology. Did you know that someone took twenty-four rabbits to Australia and now they have millions of rabbits because there are no predators to get rid of them? What if the same thing happens here? Millions of venomous spiders everywhere!" Nancy looked at Pete and Krish. "We have to find it."

"*Find* it?" Krish said, and put his glasses back on.

"Yes. Find Subject Zero," said Nancy. "Think about it: a rare spider in Crooked Oak would be a brilliant story for the Mystery Shed. And we might even stop an invasion!"

"O-OK," said Krish. "How do we do that?"

"Like this." Nancy brought up a map of Crooked Oak on her phone. She crouched between Krish and Pete so they could watch her put three markers on the map in the places where the cats had gone missing. Then she placed a fourth marker at Rose Cottage.

"The people at Rose Cottage said something about spiders hatching and spreading out, right?" Nancy asked Krish.

"Right," Krish said, realising what Nancy was doing. "And in the article it says the 'soldier' spiders fan out to hunt and bring food back to the colony."

"So?" Pete said, looking confused.

"So if we join these ..." Nancy put her finger on the screen and dragged a line from one marker to the next and the next, forming a circle.

"It should give us an idea of where the spiders are fanning out *from*," Krish finished for her.

"Exactly," Nancy agreed. "So … Oh." She stopped and stared at the screen.

Krish's mouth fell open.

Pete went white.

Dunwick Farm was at the centre of Nancy's circle.

Krish remembered the man and woman standing in the garden at Rose Cottage. The woman had said something he had forgotten about until now: that Subject Zero would be hiding somewhere "dark and sheltered". And then Krish remembered the spider husk he had found a few days ago. How could he have forgotten about it?

"It's in the barn," Krish said.

And that was when Rashmi started to scream.

CHAPTER 14

Along Came a Spider

Pete was normally the fastest, but it was Krish who raced out of AREA 51 first. He barrelled into the yard just as Gizmo started barking like crazy at the half-open barn door. Rashmi's sharp and terrified screaming was coming from inside the barn. Krish yanked the door wide and came to a sudden stop.

He stared at the nightmare before him.

The barn was cluttered with junk. An old tractor with peeling red paint was parked next to a rusted plough. Barrels and tools and broken machines lay all over the place. And everything was covered with spider webs.

Everything.

They stretched from wall to wall and floor to ceiling. They clung to the tractor and the plough, coating everything in a layer of silk. Worst of all was that Rashmi was right in the middle of it, screaming and covered in spiders. They were in her hair, on her face, clambering in and out of her clothes. Panicking, Rashmi flailed about, becoming more and more trapped in the webs they spun around her.

"Rashmi!" Krish shouted as he stepped into the barn, but as soon as he did, a wave of spiders appeared from the webs. They scuttled from under the tractor and swarmed towards him.

They were pale grey, with plump bodies about the size of Krish's thumb. Their long legs moved fast as they ran along the floor and across the webs.

They lowered from the ceiling on strands of silk. They appeared from behind old buckets. And all the time, Rashmi continued to scream.

"Get back!" Nancy warned as she grabbed Krish by the back of his shirt and dragged him out of the barn into the yard.

Pete was already out there, staring wide-eyed. His mouth was open but no words were coming out. His body sagged with fear.

Gizmo was still barking and the spiders kept coming. They surged out of the barn, pouring into the yard from the open door and squeezing through cracks in the walls. There were hundreds of them. Maybe even thousands.

"No," Pete whispered as he backed away.

"Look out!" Nancy shouted as one of the spiders stopped. It tightened its long legs as if it were crouching, then launched itself at them.

It jumped almost a metre into the air and sailed across the cobbles, closing the gap towards Nancy in a split second.

Nancy was quick to react. She twisted to one side, and the spider slipped past and plopped to the ground behind her. It narrowly missed Pete, who yelped and stumbled over Rashmi's cricket bat lying on the ground.

Still barking, Gizmo turned to face the spider as it scooted around to aim itself at them again. It tightened its legs and jumped once more, but this time Nancy was ready. She scooped Rashmi's cricket bat from the ground and swatted the spider from the air. Its plump body hit the bat with a soft "splat".

"We have to get away!" Nancy yelled.

Krish was desperate to save Rashmi, but there was no way he could reach the barn with so many spiders blocking the way.

"Back to the house!" Krish shouted.

Nancy swatted another leaping spider before she turned and ran.

Behind them, the spiders swarmed closer and closer.

Pete reached the door first, running so fast he had to put out his arms to stop himself slamming against it.

"Open it!" Pete screamed. "Open the door!" His voice was full of panic.

Krish fumbled in his pocket for his keys while Gizmo stood guard beside him.

"Open it!" Pete screamed again.

Krish yanked his keys from his pocket. They jangled in his trembling fingers as he searched for the right one.

"They're getting closer!" Nancy shouted, holding the cricket bat ready.

Krish found the right key.

"Don't drop it. Don't drop it," Krish whispered to himself. His hands were shaking so much he missed the lock, sliding the key to one side. He fumbled again, then the key slotted into place.

Krish turned the key and Pete pushed inside as soon as the door started to open. Krish went next with Gizmo at his heels, then Nancy backed in, swatting at another spider as it leapt at them. As soon as she was in, Krish slammed the door shut.

There was the pitter-patter sound of spiders hitting the door and then everything went quiet.

CHAPTER 15

A Thousand Horrors

Pete, Nancy and Krish stood in the hallway, breathing heavily, staring at the door. Gizmo stayed close.

"Spiders," Pete muttered. "Why did it have to be spiders?"

"We have to help Rashmi," Krish said. His mind raced as he tried to figure out what to do, but one thought jumped out at him. It was an awful realisation that made him turn to Nancy.

"What if this is our fault?" Krish said. "Remember when we came back from the crash site? The goats went crazy. So maybe 'Subject

Zero' came back with *us*. Maybe it climbed on to a backpack or hung on to us somehow, and then it had its babies here. Thousands of them."

"Wait ..." Pete swallowed hard, trying to find his voice. "If ... if those are the babies, then ... what does the adult look like? What does ... Oh no."

He pointed at a gangly leg pushing into the gap under the door. Another leg followed, then a plump body squeezed through. Once it was inside, the large spider turned one way then the other, as if it were searching. Its jaws opened and closed as it moved, revealing black fangs like curved needles. Fine hairs bristled on its legs. Faint fuzzy swirls and stripes were just visible on its almost translucent back.

Gizmo bared his teeth and stepped forward, but Krish grabbed him.

"Leave," Krish said to Gizmo.

When Krish spoke, it was as if the spider suddenly knew where he was. It turned towards him with a jerk, lifted its front legs and did something that was somehow worse than anything.

It hissed.

A second later, it jumped at Krish's face, its fangs bared, ready to sink them into his flesh.

"No!" Krish yelped, and lifted his arms in defence. Nancy stepped in and swung the cricket bat, whacking the spider out of the air. It smacked against the wall, leaving a wet brown mark.

Krish looked down at the broken spider and was horrified to see another one squeezing under the door.

Then another.

And another.

"Upstairs!" Krish shouted.

But when they turned, they saw something that made their blood run cold.

"Oh no," Nancy whispered. "They're already inside."

Spiders scuttled on the landing upstairs. They were all over the wall. They were on the ceiling and crawling on the bannister. And they continued to squeeze under the front door.

"We have to get out of here," Krish shouted. He took Pete's arm and dragged him along the hallway into the kitchen. Nancy followed, trying not to trip over Gizmo, who was staying close to Krish and snarling at the invaders.

The spiders swarmed after them, scurrying across the walls and over the kitchen surfaces. They scrambled on the tiles and cupboards, and their tiny legs crossed the hard surfaces, filling the kitchen with the most hideous sound.

Tick-tack-tick-tack. Tick-tack-tick-tack.

Krish ran straight to the back door. He
pulled it open and they all stumbled outside.
He slammed it shut and stopped to catch his
breath. Gizmo looked up at him as if to ask
what they were going to do now.

"We need to save Rashmi," Krish said,
breathing hard. "We need help. Has anyone
got a phone? I left mine in AREA 51."

Pete shook his head while Nancy fumbled
her phone from her pocket and grunted in
frustration. "No signal again," she said.
"Nothing at all. Not even when I call 999.
What about our bikes? We could go for help?"

Krish thought for a moment, then rushed
over to his dad's storeroom behind the house.
Close to the edge of the field, it was a small
brick building where Dad kept his tools for
fixing up the farm.

"There's no time to go for help," Krish said as he undid the bolt. "We'll have to help Rashmi ourselves."

"How?" Nancy asked.

Krish scanned the storeroom for spiders, then went inside and took three sets of thick overalls from the shelf. He also grabbed three pairs of gardening gloves and three orange hard hats.

"Put these on," Krish said, passing them to Nancy and Pete.

Pete just stood there with the protective gear in his arms.

"You have to put them on," Nancy said to Pete. She leaned the cricket bat against the wall and stepped into her overalls, pulling them over her school uniform. They were too big, but the material was thick and stiff, and might just protect her.

"Why ...?" Pete couldn't get his words out. "Spiders?"

"Come on, Pete," Krish said as he helped Pete into his overalls. "You're the brave one. You can do this."

Pete watched Krish. He took a deep breath and shuddered.

"Seriously," Krish said as he pushed his glasses up the bridge of his nose. "They're just spiders. I need you to be strong and brave like always." He put both hands on Pete's shoulders and looked right into his eyes. "*I need you*. I can't do it without you."

It was as if a light came on inside Pete. His eyes brightened.

"OK." Pete nodded. "No ... problemo."

Krish forced himself to smile. "Good," he said, and handed Pete a spade for whacking spiders. Then he pulled on his overalls, put on his hard hat and took the weed-burner from its hook on the wall.

Krish turned the valve to start the gas, then thumbed the striker switch. A soft orange flame popped into life at the end of the nozzle and Krish pressed the trigger to test it. The orange flame became a deadly cone of blue heat.

"Right," Krish said. "Let's go and save my sister."

CHAPTER 16

Nancy's Idea

Spiders were already squeezing through the crack under the back door as Krish, Nancy and Pete hurried around the side of the house. When they reached the front, Krish stopped and looked across the yard.

Dunwick Farm was infested with spiders. AREA 51 and the other outhouses were covered in them. The yard moved as if the cobbles were alive, and the hen house was full of webs. Spiders were appearing from the trees surrounding the farm, and more were scuttling down the drive.

"They're everywhere," Krish gasped.

"They're coming home," Nancy said. "To protect their queen."

"From us?" Pete asked.

"Exactly," Krish said, thinking about the spiders Nancy had killed. "They'll never let us get into the barn. There are too many of them."

"I have an idea," Nancy said quietly. "Remember how that spider in the house only went for you when you spoke to Gizmo? Well, they don't have eyes, do they? It said so in that article I read. They hunt by sound." She took her phone from her pocket and clicked the volume as high as it would go. "So, let's give them something to hunt."

Krish understood what Nancy was going to do. He crouched and pressed his face against the soft fur on Gizmo's neck. "You need to be quiet," Krish said to Gizmo. "Stay here, OK? Stay."

Nancy clicked on her music app and went to the first track she could find.

She pressed play.

The music erupted from the phone and Nancy threw it as if it were a hand grenade. It sailed through the air and landed in the weeds at the far side of the yard, close to AREA 51.

The spiders in the yard swarmed towards the sound.

"That should keep them busy," Nancy said. "But not for ever."

Pale-faced, Pete took a deep breath and nodded. "OK. Let's go."

They left Gizmo behind and edged across the yard to the barn with their weapons ready. They eased the barn door wide enough to sneak inside.

It was beautiful and nightmarish all at once. The last of the evening sun pierced the cracks in the walls, sparkling on the webs. The shadows of spiders scuttled about in the glistening silvery strands, but there were other shapes too: large masses cocooned in webs, that made Krish think of missing cats and songbirds. Probably the hens from the hen house too.

A larger cocoon hung close to the floor between the old tractor and the rusty plough, at almost the exact centre of the barn. The shape was about the size of Krish's sister, Rashmi.

Squinting past the webs was like looking into a smeary window, but Krish could just see Rashmi's face through the thin silk that covered her head.

She was only a few metres away, but it felt as if she were on the other side of the world.

Krish looked at Nancy and Pete, then pointed to his sister.

The three of them nodded to each other, then Krish raised his weed-burner and pressed the trigger. He touched the intense flame to the web in front of him and it burnt away with a crackle of sparkling embers.

The spiders went crazy.

CHAPTER 17

The Queen

Krish pressed forward, scorching away the silky curtains of web with the weed-burner. Spiders scattered in all directions. The air filled with floating embers and the sickly smell of burnt webs.

Nancy and Pete followed Krish past piles of old tyres and sheets of rusted metal. But as they burnt their way deeper into the barn using the weed-burner, the spiders became less confused. Instead of running away, they were turning to face the threat.

Nancy and Pete held their weapons ready as hundreds of spiders began to hiss at them.

Krish approached the cocoon that he knew was his sister. He saw a single spider leg rise up from behind Rashmi to rest on her shoulder. It was followed by another, then another, and an enormous spider slowly came into view.

Krish knew this must be Subject Zero. The queen.

She was bigger than any spider Krish had ever seen. Her pale grey body was larger than two of his fists together. The stubby feelers on her eyeless face, called pedipalps, moved gently up and down as she climbed up onto Rashmi's shoulder. Three of the queen's long, bristly legs stretched out over Rashmi's head. She lifted her pedipalps to reveal large, curved fangs as long as Krish's little finger.

Every instinct in Krish's body screamed at him to run. He knew that if the queen attacked him, she would sink her fangs into his skin. His overalls might be thick enough to protect him

from the smaller spiders, but the queen would be stronger. Her venom would be deadly.

But he had to save Rashmi.

The queen hissed and rocked back on her long legs. Outside, the music from Nancy's phone continued, but the spiders must have grown used to it because they were scuttling back into the barn, cutting off any escape route.

Krish looked at his friends and saw fear in their eyes.

And then the spiders attacked.

*

The first spider to leap at them missed, but others began to jump. In an instant, it was raining spiders.

Pete came to the left of Krish, swinging his spade to swat spiders from the air as they jumped at him. On Krish's right, Nancy did the same with her cricket bat.

The queen was furious, baring her fangs, ready to strike. She must have known her spiderlings were being squashed and crushed. She turned left and right, confused by the sounds around her. She didn't know where to attack, but when Krish pressed the trigger on the weed-burner, she turned towards the rushing sound of blue fire.

Krish wondered if he could stop the queen. She looked so big and powerful. But then the barn echoed with the sound of barking and suddenly Gizmo was at Krish's side.

The queen jerked in Gizmo's direction and propelled herself at him.

She was quick and strong.

But Krish was quicker.

As the queen came at Gizmo, Krish lifted the burner and aimed the flame straight at her.

The queen screamed the most awful high-pitched sound. Krish had never imagined a spider could make such a noise. It was the sound of pain and frustration and fear.

The air was suddenly filled with the stink of burning hair as the bristles on the queen's legs caught fire. She dropped to the ground, screaming and hissing as she scuttled in circles.

Gizmo raced out of the barn while the spiderlings swarmed towards their queen as if to protect her, abandoning their attack on Krish and his friends. But the queen was already aflame and clambered over a pile of old dry hay that immediately caught fire. Flames burst upwards, burning away the webs and any spiderlings caught in the heat.

The fire spread in an instant. It leapt from the hay to a pile of old wood. Smoke began to fill the barn.

"Rashmi!" Krish shouted, and his friends knew what he meant.

They pushed forward and ripped open the cocoon in front of them. Together they dragged Rashmi out and turned towards the exit.

The smoke was thickening. Krish's eyes stung and began to stream with tears. He coughed away the suffocating smoke. Already it was too thick to see properly in the barn.

"Stick together!" Nancy spluttered.

Pete and Krish kept of hold of Rashmi, carrying her through the smoke as Nancy led the way. Finally, they burst out of the barn door and collapsed into the fresh air, their eyes stinging and lungs burning.

CHAPTER 18

Choose Wisely

Half an hour later, the sun had set, but the yard was ablaze with blue and red flashing lights.

Krish watched the paramedics lift Rashmi into the ambulance. She was strapped to a stretcher, with her eyes closed and an oxygen mask over her face. Krish asked to go with her, but the paramedics told him to stay with the police, then they closed the ambulance doors and drove away with a blast from its siren.

Pete and Nancy stood in the yard with Krish, each of them huddled in a blanket. Gizmo sat beside them, panting as if he'd just been for a long walk.

The yard was covered with filthy water. The air stank of burnt wood. Firefighters were reeling in hoses and returning equipment to the fire engine. A police officer stood by the front door to the house and two others were at the far side of the yard. Behind Krish, the barn was a scorched and smoking mess.

"We've been in touch with each of your parents," said a voice that startled Krish from his thoughts.

Krish turned to look at the police officer who'd spoken. She was standing beside him wearing a yellow high-viz jacket. She had dark hair and kind eyes, and had introduced herself as "Officer Myers".

"Your mum and dad are going straight to the hospital," Officer Myers told Krish. "But Nancy's parents are coming here, so you can go with them for now." She looked at Pete and said, "They will take *you* home to your mum."

In a daze, the three of them nodded.

"So," Officer Myers went on, flipping open her notebook. "I'm trying to make sense of your story. *What* were you saying about spiders?"

"They were everywhere," Pete said. "They—"

Before Pete could say more, Officer Myers' radio let out a sharp burst of static and a voice spoke from it.

"*Someone here to see you, Officer Myers.*"

Officer Myers smiled and said, "I won't be a moment." She walked back to the police car at the entrance to Dunwick Farm.

As Officer Myers crossed the yard, Krish noticed a black Range Rover parked on the road outside. Then two people appeared from the darkness behind it – a man and a woman, both wearing black suits. They approached Officer Myers.

"It's them," Krish whispered. "The ones from Rose Cottage."

The man and woman spoke to Officer Myers, then headed for the three children huddled in blankets.

"We're in trouble," Nancy said.

Krish had an awful feeling deep in his stomach. He felt so sick he thought he might throw up. There was something sinister about these people. Something that made his skin crawl even more than the spiders.

The man and woman stopped and looked down at the children as if they were studying them. Then the woman smiled. It wasn't a pleasant smile. It was as if she had forgotten how to smile properly.

Gizmo growled.

"You have two options," the woman said in a low voice. "In Option A, you tell the police about the spiders, no one believes you, and they blame you for the fire." She leaned over them. "Everyone would think you're lying. Even your parents. Trust me – we'd make sure of that."

Pete, Nancy and Krish didn't know what to say.

"Do you know what happens to liars?" the woman continued. "They get punished. And their sisters don't recover from mysterious illnesses. You wouldn't want that, would you?"

Krish shook his head. He couldn't believe it. The woman was telling them to keep quiet. She was threatening Rashmi!

The man put a hand on the woman's arm and stopped her. When he smiled, it looked more real.

"In Option B," the man said, "we make sure everyone believes this was an accident. An electrical fault, perhaps. The fire was an accident and you saved your sister." He fixed his eyes on Krish. "The three of you would be heroes and your father would get a new barn. And your sister would make a full recovery, of course. Trust me – we'd make sure of that."

The man smiled again and stepped back so he was standing next to the woman.

"Option A or Option B," the woman said. "Choose wisely."

CHAPTER 19

Cover-Up

A few days later, Krish was standing at the window in AREA 51, staring out at the burnt remains of the barn. He and Pete and Nancy had been off school since the fire, but now they were together again in AREA 51. The room smelled of the pizza his mum had ordered from Deodato's Pizzeria.

"Those people must have been from BGen," Krish said, remembering the man and woman in dark suits. "They shouldn't have taken that spider from the cave in Brazil and they shouldn't have lost control of it, so now they've covered it all up."

"And they made us help them," Nancy complained. She was slouched on a blue beanbag, nibbling a pizza crust. Gizmo was sitting in front of her, drooling. "They took that poor spider from its home and brought it here and we had to ..." Nancy couldn't bring herself to say it.

"Kill it," Krish said. "I feel bad about that. It was only being itself."

"They should never have brought the spider here," Nancy said.

"But they did it for the right reason," Pete argued. He was standing by the printer while it whizzed and chugged. "They were trying to use its venom to make a medicine to help people with bad pain, right? People like my mum."

"But what if those spiders spread all over the country?" Nancy said. "Imagine an 'invasive species' like that!"

Pete sighed. He knew Nancy was right. But, in a way, he thought he was right too.

"Anyway, you had no choice," Pete told Krish. "You had to kill it. Imagine if it had bitten you. And we had no choice about helping the BGen people cover it up, either. They were scary. I reckon it was them messing with the phone signal. People like that carry jammers in their cars, you know."

The printer stopped printing and Pete held up the sheet of paper.

"Anyway, look," Pete said. "We're heroes."

Pete had printed an article from the local news about them rescuing Rashmi from a barn fire. Pete pinned it on the noticeboard beside an article about Mrs Hudson, "a keen gardener and Biology teacher at Crooked Oak School". It explained how she caught a rare sleeping virus after pricking her finger on a rose thorn. There was another article about people finding

dead spiders in their sheds and garages –
mysterious spiders that were unlike anything
people had ever seen before.

Nancy rolled her eyes. "I hate those
articles. *We* know what those spiders are and
we know Mrs Hudson was bitten by one, but we
can't say anything."

"Or maybe we can," Krish said, taking a
slice of pepperoni pizza from the box on the
desk. "We can write a story for the Mystery
Shed. We just have to leave out some of the
details."

Just then, the door banged open and Rashmi
burst in. Outside, the birds were singing.

Krish smiled at his sister and said, "What's
up?"

Rashmi looked surprised. "What? You're
not going to shout at me? Tell me to leave you
alone?"

"Nope." Krish took a bite of pizza. "Maybe next time."

Rashmi looked at Nancy. "Who's he and what have you done with my brother?"

Nancy couldn't help laughing.

"Do you want to come out and play cricket?" Rashmi asked. "I'll let you all bat first."

"All right," Krish said. "We'll be out in a minute."

When Rashmi was gone, Nancy said, "Rashmi doesn't remember anything?"

"Nothing," Krish confirmed. "She doesn't even remember going into the barn."

"Weird," Nancy said. She threw her pizza crust to Gizmo, who caught it with a "snap".

"One thing," Pete said. "I was wondering about the spiders people have been finding in their sheds and garages. Why are they all dead?"

"We found some here too," Krish told him. "Ones that must have got away from the fire but not lived for much longer. Maybe they can't survive without their queen. Once Subject Zero died, they *all* died."

"Maybe," Nancy said. "Or maybe this is just the wrong environment for these spiders. Maybe they just can't survive in Crooked Oak."

"Or maybe," Krish added, "it's just one mystery we'll never be able to answer."

Our books are tested
for children and young people by
children and young people.

Thanks to everyone who consulted on
a manuscript for their time and effort in
helping us to make our books better
for our readers.